SPORTS GREATS

TOP 10 GAMES IN FOOTBALL

DAVID ARETHA

Enslow Publishing
101 W. 23rd Street
Suite 240
New York, NY 10011
USA
enslow.com

Published in 2017 by Enslow Publishing, LLC.
101 W. 23rd Street, Suite 240, New York, NY 10011

Library of Congress Cataloging-in-Publication Data

Names: Aretha, David, author.
Title: Top 10 games in football / Dave Aretha.
Other titles: Top ten games in football
Description: New York : Enslow Publishing, LLC, 2017 | Series: Sports greats | Includes bibliographical references and index.
Identifiers: LCCN 2016022708 | ISBN 9780766083141 (Library Bound) | ISBN 9780766083127 (Paperback) | ISBN 9780766083134 (6-pack)
Subjects: LCSH: Football—United States—History—Juvenile literature. | Football—United States—Miscellanea—Juvenile literature.
Classification: LCC GV950.7 .A79 2017 | DDC 796.330973—dc23
LC record available at https://lccn.loc.gov/2016022708

Printed in China

To Our Readers: We have done our best to make sure all website addresses in this book were active and appropriate when we went to press. However, the author and the publisher have no control over and assume no liability for the material available on those websites or on any websites they may link to. Any comments or suggestions can be sent by e-mail to customerservice@enslow.com.

Photo Credits: Cover, p. 1 Joe Robbins/Getty Images Sport/Getty Images; pp. 4–5, Andy Hayt/Sports Illustrated/Getty Images; p. 8 Hy Peskin/Sports Illustrated/Getty Images; pp. 10–11, 17, 26–27, 41, 45 © AP Images; p. 13 Marvin Newman/Sports Illustrated/Getty Images; p. 15 Bob Leverone/Sporting News via Getty Images; pp. 18–19 John Biever/Sports Illustrated/Getty Images; pp. 21, 42–43 Kevin C. Cox/Getty Images Sport/Getty Images; pp. 22–23 Andy Lyons/Getty Images Sport/Getty Images; p. 25 Focus on Sport/Getty Images Sport/Getty Images; p. 29 Ronald C. Modra /Sports Illustrated/Getty Images; pp. 30–31 Rich Clarkson/Sports Illustrated/Getty Images; p. 32 Bill Frakes/Sports Illustrated/Getty Images; pp. 34–35 Rob Gauthier/Los Angeles Times via Getty Images; p. 37 Ron Jenkins/Fort Worth Star-Telegram/MCT via Getty Images; pp. 38–39 Steve Grayson/WireImage/Getty Images; design elements throughout book: maodoltee/Shutterstock.com (football field), RTimages/Shutterstock.com (grass), EsraKeskinSenay/Shutterstock.com (football stadium), Prixel Creative/Shutterstock.com (football play).

Contents

Introduction 4

1958 NFL Championship Game 7

1967 NFL Championship Game 10

Super Bowl XLII 14

Super Bowl XLIII 18

Super Bowl XLIX 22

1984 Orange Bowl 26

2003 Fiesta Bowl 30

2006 Rose Bowl 34

2007 Fiesta Bowl 38

2013 "Iron Bowl" 42

Glossary 46

Further Reading 47

Index 48

INTRODUCTION

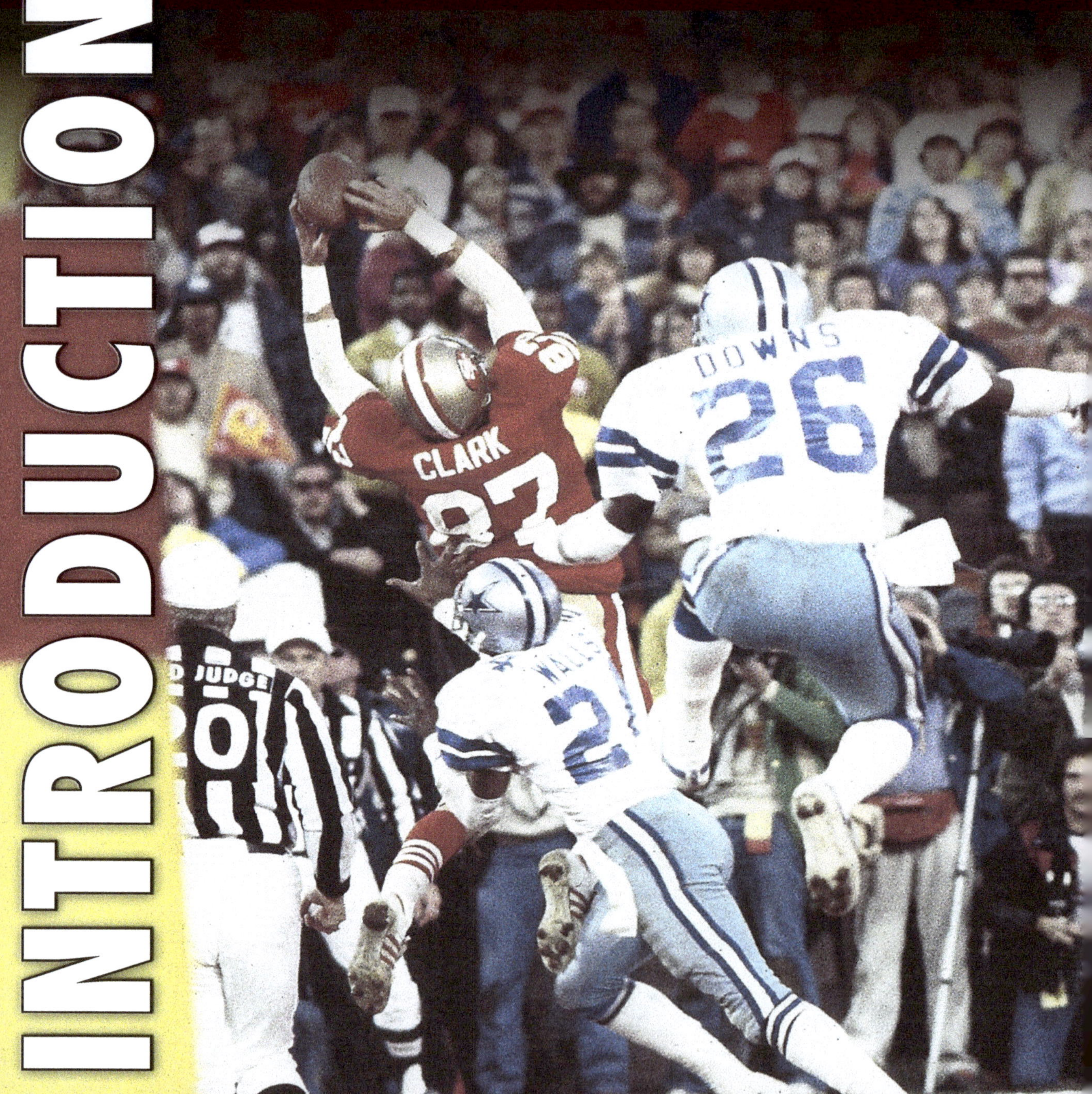

San Francisco's Dwight Clark makes "the Catch"—one of the most famous plays in NFL history. Joe Montana's last-minute pass spelled defeat for Dallas in the NFC Championship Game in January 1982.

Buffalo Bills fans had given up. On January 3, 1993, Houston safety Bubba McDowell returned an interception 58 yards for a touchdown. That put the Oilers up 35–3 in the third quarter, and Bills fans headed for the exits. "We [still] had a chance," said Bills coach Marv Levy. "About the same chance as a guy has of winning the New York Lottery."

The Bills were playing with backup quarterback Frank Reich, but in the second half he emerged as a hero. Reich drove Buffalo downfield for a touchdown to cut the deficit to 35–10. Next, he fired a 38-yard scoring pass to Don Beebe. Then, incredibly, he threw three touchdown passes to star receiver Andre Reed. Buffalo erased a 32-point deficit and now led 38–35.

As this stunning comeback took place, the Bills fans who had left tried to get back into the stadium. Many begged ticket takers to let them in, while others tried to climb the fences surrounding the field.

Houston tied the game with a field goal, but Buffalo prevailed in overtime 41–38. It was one of the greatest games in NFL history...but not quite good enough to be featured in this book.

Quarterback Joe Montana won two of the most incredible contests ever played. In the 1981 NFC Championship Game, Montana fired a last-minute touchdown pass to Dwight Clark to defeat Dallas 28–27. "Joe Cool" was being chased toward the sideline, and his pass looked like it would sail out of the end zone. But Clark soared to the heavens to make what is still known as "the Catch."

Three years earlier, Montana performed his magic for Notre Dame University in the Cotton Bowl. It was freezing in Dallas, and Montana was sick with the flu. During halftime, he ate chicken soup while wrapped in warm blankets. The University of Houston was leading 34–12 in the fourth quarter when Montana found his inner strength. In the final seven and a half minutes, he led the Fighting Irish to three touchdowns and a pair of two-point conversions. His TD pass to Kris Haines as time expired tied the game, and the extra point by Joe Unis won it.

It would forever be known as the "Chicken Soup Game." Or as sportswriter Steve Wulf wrote, the game featured "an Italian leading the Irish to triumph thanks to a traditional Jewish remedy." It was hard to top that contest, but the battles featured in this book actually did. Grab a bowl of soup and enjoy the 10 greatest football games ever played.

1958 NFL CHAMPIONSHIP GAME

KEY PLAYER: JOHNNY UNITAS
TEAM: BALTIMORE COLTS
OPPONENT: NEW YORK GIANTS
SETTING: NEW YORK CITY, DECEMBER 28, 1958

Steve Myhra had grown up in a desolate place, where milking the cow was often the highlight of the day. Now he was in a completely different environment. It was the 1958 NFL Championship in New York City. Some 64,000 fans focused on him in Yankee Stadium, and tons more watched with keen interest on television.

Myhra, the Baltimore Colts' kicker, was about to attempt a 20-yard field goal with 10 seconds left in the fourth quarter. If he made it, the Colts and New York Giants would be tied at 17–17. "I told myself I better not miss it," Myhra said, "or it would be a long, cold winter back on the farm in North Dakota." Myhra made it, and—for the first time in NFL history—a game was headed to overtime.

In the late 1950s, millions of Americans were buying televisions for the first time. The 1958 NFL Championship Game attracted approximately 45 million viewers, by far the most ever for a football game.

Baltimore quarterback Johnny Unitas displays his picture-perfect throwing motion during the "Greatest Game Ever Played." Johnny U threw for 349 yards that day.

The Colts featured quarterback Johnny Unitas. Three years earlier, Johnny U was playing in a semipro league for $6 a game. Now he was the "Golden Arm"—a supreme leader and a First Team All-Pro. The Giants countered with the league's best defense, led by future Hall of Famers Sam Huff (linebacker) and Rosey Brown (lineman).

In frigid weather, the teams combined for eight fumbles. Giants running back Frank Gifford, who would become a longtime broadcaster for *Monday Night Football*, fumbled twice in the first half. The Colts converted both into eventual touchdowns. At halftime, Baltimore led 14–3.

In the third quarter, New Yorkers finally had something to cheer about. Quarterback Charlie Conerly threw to Kyle Rote, who rambled downfield. Rote fumbled but teammate Alex Webster picked up the ball and took it to the 1-yard line. The Giants scored and trailed 14–10 entering the fourth quarter.

More fans gathered around their TV sets as the action heated up. Conerly completed a 46-yard pass to tight end Bob Schnelker. Then, Gifford made up for his fumbles by hauling in a 15-yard touchdown pass. New York now led 17–14.

With minutes frittering away, the Colts twice entered field goal range. But they missed a field goal and later got sacked outside of field goal range. Finally, they started a drive with 1:56 remaining at their own 14-yard line. Cool and confident, Unitas went to work. He completed three consecutive passes (25, 15, and 22 yards) to his favorite receiver, Raymond Berry. Those completions put the ball on the 13, and Myhra booted his game-tying field goal.

In overtime, the Giants punted on their first possession. Unitas twice completed third-and-long passes to keep Baltimore's drive going. After 12 plays, the Colts had the ball on the Giants' 1-yard line. From there, 220-pound fullback Alan Ameche powered in for the score. Ameche called it "probably the shortest run I ever made—and the most remembered." Afterward, NBC announcer Chris Schenkel stated that, "this is going to go down as the greatest game ever played."

1967 NFL CHAMPIONSHIP GAME

KEY PLAYER: BART STARR

TEAM: GREEN BAY PACKERS

OPPONENT: DALLAS COWBOYS

SETTING: GREEN BAY, WISCONSIN, DECEMBER 31, 1967

On the morning of the 1967 NFL Championship Game, Dan Reeves and Walt Garrison were freezing. In Appleton, Wisconsin, the two Dallas Cowboys walked and then ran to a nearby restaurant. "Dang, it's cold out there," Reeves said when he arrived. "Well it ought to be," a woman replied. "It's 17 below zero."

Even for northern Wisconsin, this was freakishly cold. By game time the temperature had risen to -13 Fahrenheit, but 15-mile-per-hour winds made it feel like 38 below. Green Bay coach Vince Lombardi had ordered the installation of heating coils beneath the playing surface. But the system didn't work, and the field was frozen solid. "Our field was full of ruts and divots," said

Packers offensive lineman Jerry Kramer. "When you went down, it was like falling on a jagged concrete surface."

Bundling up, 50,000 loyal Packers fans packed Lambeau Field. The winner of this game would win the NFL Championship and then meet the champion of the American Football League in the Super Bowl. This game would forever be known as the "Ice Bowl."

How cold was it? It was so cold that when referee Norm Schacter blew the whistle for the opening kickoff,

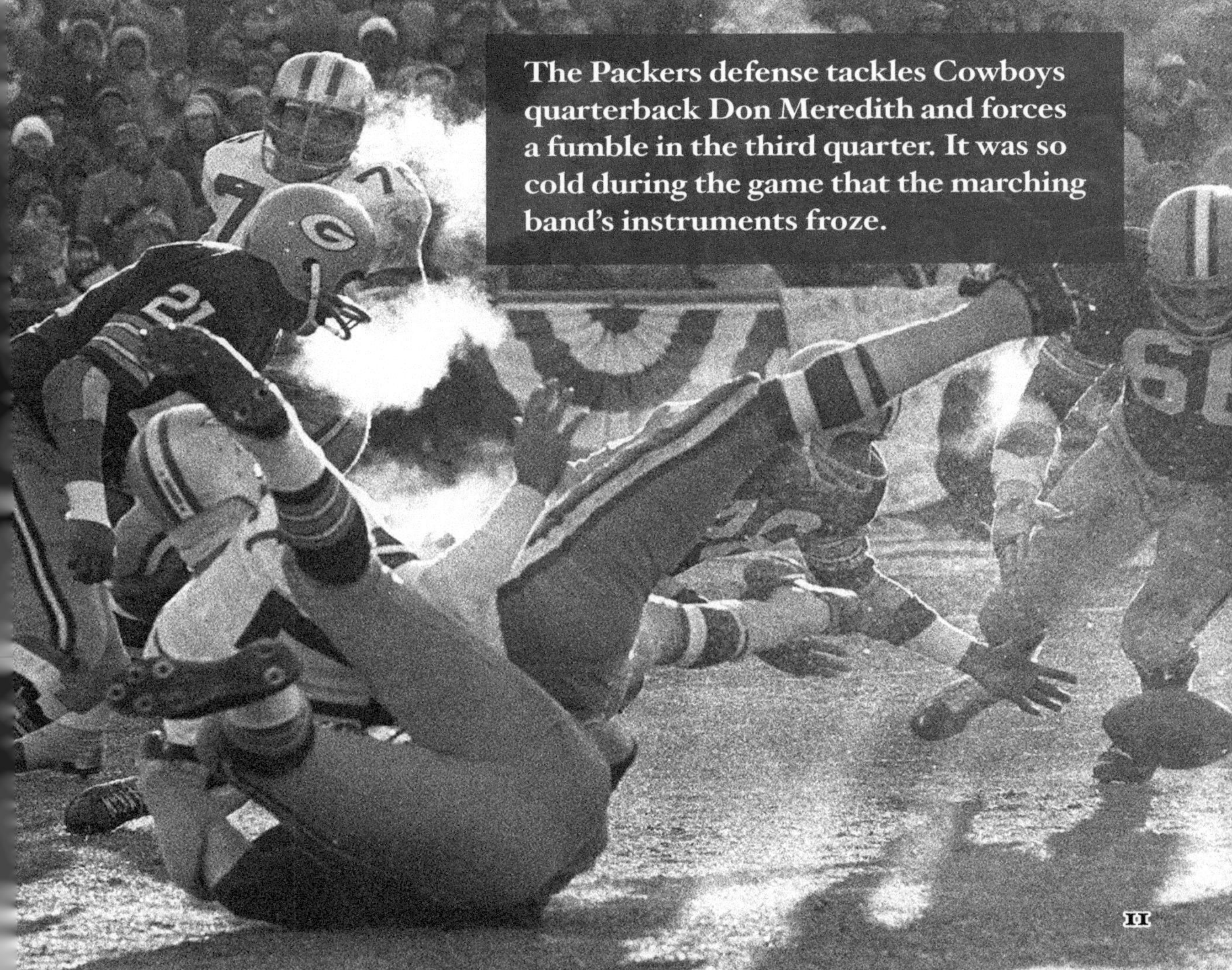

The Packers defense tackles Cowboys quarterback Don Meredith and forces a fumble in the third quarter. It was so cold during the game that the marching band's instruments froze.

it literally froze to his lips. They played the rest of the game without whistles.

While the team from Texas was frozen stiff, the Packers dominated early. Bart Starr threw 8-yard and 46-yard touchdown passes to Boyd Dowler, and Green Bay led 14–0 in the second quarter. Then the momentum turned. Dallas's George Andrie scooped up a fumble and returned it 7 yards for a touchdown. The Cowboys added a field goal, and Dallas's Reeves completed a 50-yard scoring pass to Lance Rentzel early in the fourth quarter. The Cowboys now led 17–14.

As the sun dropped, the game was played in shadows. The temperature fell to -19 and the wind chill to -50. "I'm going to take a bite of my coffee," CBS broadcaster Frank Gifford said. Packers linebacker Ray Nitschke developed frostbite on his feet. Starr had frostbite on his fingers, adding to the legend of his team's final drive.

With 4:50 remaining and still trailing 17–14, the Packers began the drive from their own 32-yard line. After a successful mix of short passes and runs, they moved the ball to the 1-yard line. That's where they stalled. On the next two plays, running back Donny Anderson slipped on the frozen turf and couldn't score. It was now third-and-goal at the 1 with 16 seconds remaining. The Packers called a time-out.

Everyone expected a pass because if it fell incomplete, the clock would stop. That would allow

Packers quarterback Bart Starr sneaks into the end zone with the game-winning touchdown. The field was so frozen that he and coach Vince Lombardi didn't trust the running backs with the ball.

Green Bay to run another play—including a possible field goal to tie the score.

During the time-out, Lombardi and Starr discussed a running play. The QB didn't want to give the ball to a running back because he felt he would slip again. Instead, Starr wanted to carry it himself. "Run it, and let's get the [heck] out of here!" Lombardi declared.

Starr took the snap, ducked his head, and plowed into the end zone. The Packers won the Ice Bowl 21–17. Two weeks later, they crushed Oakland 33–14 in the Super Bowl in Miami...where it was a comfy 68 degrees.

SUPER BOWL XLII
KEY PLAYER: ELI MANNING
TEAM: NEW YORK GIANTS
OPPONENT: NEW ENGLAND PATRIOTS
SETTING: GLENDALE, ARIZONA, FEBRUARY 3, 2008

The rock group Tom Petty and the Heartbreakers performed during halftime of Super Bowl XLII. But the real heroes of this game were Eli Manning and his "heartbreakers." Manning's Giants broke the hearts of the New England Patriots, who were looking to become the first 19–0 team in NFL history.

More than 97 million American TV viewers—a new record—tuned in to watch this historic matchup. It was a classic "David vs. Goliath" battle. The Giants had snuck into the play-offs with a 10–6 record. They won three play-off games, all on the road, to reach the Super Bowl.

Meanwhile, the Patriots became the first team in history to go 16–0 during the regular season. Behind mastermind coach Bill Belichick, the Patriots opened the season with eight blowout victories. They finished with an NFL-record 589 points, and they allowed just 274. NFL MVP Tom Brady threw a league-record 50

Critics said that Eli Manning wasn't a strong enough leader to marshal the Giants to the ultimate title. Against New England, he proved them wrong by winning the Super Bowl MVP Award—his first of two.

touchdown passes, and spectacular wide receiver Randy Moss set a new NFL mark with 23 TD catches.

The Patriots entered the Super Bowl as a two-touchdown favorite. Many experts, though, felt this might be a closer game. After all, in the regular season finale, New England survived a 38–35 scare against New York. Recalled Patriots safety Rodney Harrison, "I wouldn't say doubt crept in that night, but I wondered, 'Are we beatable?'"

Eli Manning, kid brother of superstar QB Peyton Manning, quarterbacked the Giants' offense. Their 10-minute drive to open the game resulted in just a field goal, but at least it kept Brady's offense off the field. Meanwhile, the Giants created a variety of defensive plays to confuse and frustrate Brady. Defensive end Justin Tuck had two sacks and a forced fumble. Through three quarters, New England managed only a 7–3 lead.

Prior to the 2007 season, Manning had been criticized for not being a strong leader. In the fourth quarter, he silenced all doubters. With 11:05 remaining, Manning capped an 80-yard drive with a 5-yard scoring pass to wide receiver David Tyree. Stunningly, the Giants led 10–7.

Legendary for his comebacks, Brady responded with his own 80-yard touchdown drive. He completed a 6-yard scoring pass to Moss, and New England led 14–10 with 2:45 left on the clock. Fans across the nation were on edge. Were the Patriots on the verge of completing the ultimate perfect season? Or could Manning pull off the greatest Super Bowl upset of all time?

With 1:15 to go, the Giants were in trouble. They faced third-and-five at their own 44, and Manning endured a heavy rush. Three Patriots got their hands on Manning, but he somehow escaped. He then tossed a wobbly pass deep downfield that Tyree had to leap high to reach. He barely caught it, then pressed it down to the top of his

Wide receiver David Tyree makes the famous "Helmet Catch" to keep the Giants' hopes alive. He held the ball against his head until after he was tackled by Patriots safety Rodney Harrison.

helmet. Even while being tackled, Tyree somehow held the ball in that position. First down at the 24.

Then, at the 13, with 45 seconds left, Manning found Plaxico Burress alone in the left corner of the end zone. Touchdown, Giants! Burress kneeled to say a quick prayer, then pumped his index finger in the air. David, not Goliath, was No. 1.

"We shocked the world," said New York linebacker Antonio Pierce. And broke some hearts. Final score: New York 17, Patriots 14.

SUPER BOWL XLIII

KEY PLAYER: SANTONIO HOLMES
TEAM: PITTSBURGH STEELERS
OPPONENT: ARIZONA CARDINALS
SETTING: TAMPA, FLORIDA, FEBRUARY 1, 2009

Good thing the Steelers were tough in 2008. They had to be because they faced the strongest schedule anyone had ever seen. Not one of their 10 non-division opponents had a losing record in 2007. Pittsburgh had to play New England (16–0 the previous season) and the New York Giants (reigning Super Bowl champions).

Fortunately for head coach Mike Tomlin, the Steelers boasted the NFL's strongest defense in 2008. With 16 sacks and 7 forced fumbles, linebacker James Harrison earned NFL Defensive Player of the Year honors. All-Pro safety Troy Polamalu—famous for his long, flowing hair—picked off seven passes.

Despite their stiff competition, the Steelers went 12–4. They beat

the rival Baltimore Ravens three times, including in the AFC Championship Game. Steelers wide receiver Hines Ward described the brutality of the Pittsburgh-Baltimore rivalry. “Sometimes guys get hit so hard, you don’t know if they’re going to get up,” he said.

In the Super Bowl, Pittsburgh faced the 9–7 Arizona Cardinals, who had scored a whopping 427 points during the season but had given up 426. Quarterback Kurt

James Harrison of the Steelers collapses after huffing and puffing 100 yards to the end zone. At the time, it was the longest touchdown play in Super Bowl history.

Warner, who had worked in a grocery store prior to his rise to NFL fame, powered the Cardinals' offense. The 99 million Americans who watched this game were in for a treat.

Pittsburgh led 10–7, but anticipation built before halftime—and not just because singer Bruce Springsteen was about to perform. Arizona had the ball on the Steelers' 1-yard line with 18 seconds to go. That's when Harrison intercepted a pass at the goal line and rumbled down the right sideline. Plowing over some opponents, dancing around others, Harrison stormed 100 yards for a touchdown. "It's the longest play in Super Bowl history!" blared ABC announcer Al Michaels. "A 100-yard interception return!" Harrison was so exhausted, he lay in the end zone for two minutes. Yet, a fiercely contested second half remained.

Down 20–7 in the fourth quarter, the Cardinals roared back. On one drive, Warner completed four passes to his favorite receiver, Larry Fitzgerald. The last one resulted in a touchdown with 7:41 remaining. With 3:04 to go, the Steelers committed a holding penalty in their own zone. By rule that's a safety, and now Arizona trailed by just four, 20–16. Seconds later, Fitzgerald caught a pass over the middle and blazed to the end zone for a 64-yard touchdown. Just like that, Arizona led 23–20.

But the Steelers weren't done. Quarterback Ben Roethlisberger, famous for his toughness in the clutch, marched Pittsburgh down the field. With under a

Santonio Holmes reaches out of bounds — but keeps his feet inbounds — to snatch the game-winning touchdown pass.

minute left, "Big Ben" and spectacular receiver Santonio Holmes hooked up for a 40-yard pass-and-run. Holmes reached the 6-yard line, and after an incompletion that's where the ball remained.

On the next play, Roethlisberger fired to Holmes in the right corner of the end zone. Holmes had to soar high and twist his body out of bounds to reach the ball. But somehow, his feet landed in the end zone. He then threw his arms up in victory. "All I did was [stand] up on my toes and [extend] my hands," Holmes said. Replays confirmed the extraordinary touchdown, and Pittsburgh prevailed 27–23.

"Was that a 60-minute game, or what?" exclaimed Steelers linebacker James Farrior. "It came down to the last play, and we made it."

SUPER BOWL XLIX

KEY PLAYER: MALCOLM BUTLER
TEAM: NEW ENGLAND PATRIOTS
OPPONENT: SEATTLE SEAHAWKS
SETTING: PHOENIX, ARIZONA, FEBRUARY 1, 2015

Seattle trailed in Super Bowl XLIX 28–24 with just 26 seconds remaining. Yet it seemed certain the Seahawks would win the game. They had the ball on New England's 1-yard line—and they had "Beast Mode," Marshawn Lynch. The powerful running back was a human battering ram. Certainly he would score on the next play.

New England cornerback Malcolm Butler thought his team was about to lose. "Most definitely," said Butler, an undrafted rookie from a small college. "Just like everybody else." Little did Butler know that he himself would be the hero.

The end of Super Bowl XLIX was viewed by 120 million Americans, making it the most-watched TV program of all time.

The game featured the Seahawks, reigning Super Bowl champions, against the Patriots and quarterback Tom Brady, who was playing in his record sixth Super Bowl. Yet controversy swirled over the handsome QB's head. Reportedly, Brady had been involved in under-inflating footballs for the AFC Championship Game. Such balls are easier to throw and catch. The NFL was still examining this "Deflategate" crisis, but many viewed Brady as a cheater until proven innocent.

New England's Malcolm Butler breaks up this pass with 1:10 remaining. But somehow, Jermaine Kearse manages to kick, bobble, and catch the ball for a stunning completion.

Entering the fourth quarter of the Super Bowl, Brady had bigger concerns. His team trailed 24–14, and they faced the best defense in the NFL. Brady would have to throw against the "Legion of Boom" secondary, which featured First Team All-Pros Richard Sherman and Earl Thomas as well as Pro Bowl selection Kam Chancellor.

But never underestimate Tom Brady. "He's the greatest quarterback on the planet," said teammate Julian Edelman after the game. Brady led New England on a 68-yard touchdown drive to cut the score to 24–21 with 8:00 to go. After a Seahawks punt, Brady completed all nine of his passes in another scoring drive, capped by a three-yard TD pass to Edelman. The Patriots led 28–24 with 2:06 remaining.

Now the pressure fell on young Seahawks quarterback Russell Wilson. On the first play from scrimmage, he tossed to Beast Mode, who rampaged 31 yards downfield. Later, Wilson fired a 33-yard pass toward Jermaine Kearse at the 5-yard line. Kearse and Butler soared high for the ball, each getting their fingers on it. While Kearse fell to the ground, the ball banged off each of his legs and then bounced off his hands—and then he grabbed it. "Unbe-*liev*-able!" exclaimed NBC commentator Cris Collinsworth.

It was one of the greatest plays in Super Bowl history, but it would soon be forgotten. After a 4-yard run by Lynch, Seattle had the ball on the 1-yard line with 26 ticks left. Everyone thought Lynch would get the ball again—which is why Seahawks coach Pete Carroll called

With seconds remaining, New England's Malcolm Butler sneaks in front of wide receiver Ricardo Lockette to intercept Russell Wilson's pass and win the game.

for a pass. Wilson dropped back and rifled the ball at the goal line to wide receiver Ricardo Lockette. But Butler, anticipating the pass, arrived at the ball a millisecond before Lockette did. The two players crashed into each other, and "the pass is intercepted at the goal line by Malcolm Butler!" screamed NBC's Al Michaels.

Carroll was heavily criticized for not letting Lynch carry the ball. But "Seattle's last play was Russell Wilson's fault, not Pete Carroll's," declared *USA Today*.

Brady won the game's MVP Award, but New England had a new star. Malcolm Butler had single-handedly won the Super Bowl.

1984 ORANGE BOWL

KEY PLAYER: KEN CALHOUN

TEAM: MIAMI HURRICANES

OPPONENT: NEBRASKA CORNHUSKERS

SETTING: MIAMI, FLORIDA, JANUARY 2, 1984

They called it the fumblerooski. "When the play came in from the sideline, I was kind of shocked," Nebraska guard Dean Steinkuhler told ABC Sports. "But I just said, 'Here we go.'"

It was the 1984 Orange Bowl, with 11–0 Nebraska facing 10–1 Miami for the national championship. Miami led 17–0 in the second quarter, but the Cornhuskers had the ball on the Hurricanes' 19-yard line. Quarterback Turner Gill took the snap and intentionally dropped the ball. With Miami oblivious to the fumble, Steinkuhler picked it up and ran for the touchdown. It was just one highlight of one of the greatest games ever played.

Nebraska and Miami took very different paths to the Orange Bowl. Coach

Tom Osborne's Cornhuskers beat Minnesota 84–13, and against Colorado they scored 7 touchdowns in 12 minutes, winning 69–19. Their legendary backfield featured Heisman Trophy–winning running back Mike Rozier, Heisman finalist Turner Gill, and wingback Irving Fryar—the number one overall pick in the 1984 NFL Draft.

While Nebraska ranked number one in the polls the entire season, Miami entered the year unranked.

Nebraska guard Dean Steinkuhler, the best offensive lineman in football in 1983, races to the end zone on the fumblerooski.

They then lost their opening game 28–3 to Florida. But coach Howard Schnellenberger—who wore a sport jacket, tie, and handkerchief during games—kept his players focused. With an athletic, ferocious defense, the Hurricanes won the rest of their contests.

The Huskers entered the nighttime Orange Bowl as a 10-point favorite, but the hometown crowd fired up the Hurricanes. Rifle-armed freshman Bernie Kosar threw two touchdown passes to Glenn Dennison in the first quarter, and a field goal made it 17–0 Miami.

But this was a game of huge momentum swings. Following the fumblerooski, Nebraska scored twice more to tie the game at 17–17 early in the third quarter. Then Miami roared ahead. Alonzo Highsmith leaped over the pile for a touchdown, and Albert Bentley ran for another score. The 'Canes led 31–17.

Things looked bleak for Nebraska, especially when Rozier left the game with an injury. Backup Jeff Smith, though, became the latest Huskers hero. He scored with 6:55 left to cut Miami's lead to 31–24. Over the remaining minutes, hearts pounded hard in the Orange Bowl.

Following a missed Miami field goal, Gill marched the Huskers downfield. On fourth-and-eight at the 24, Gill pitched the ball to Davis, who ran for a touchdown. Just 48 seconds remained, and Nebraska trailed 31–30.

The extra point would have tied the score, and the game likely would have ended in a 31–31 tie. (Overtime didn't exist in college football back then.) With the tie,

Alonzo Highsmith leaps over the pile to give Miami a 23–17 lead in the second half. Many more dramatic plays would follow.

number-one-ranked Nebraska still would have won the national title. But, "I don't think you go for a tie in that case," said Coach Osborne, Nebraska's esteemed head coach from 1973 to 1997. "You try to win the game. We wanted an undefeated season and a clear-cut national championship."

Thus, Nebraska tried a two-point conversion. Gill threw to Smith in the right corner of the end zone. But Ken Calhoun, who had played a great game all night, slapped the ball away. Fans poured onto the field to celebrate the stunning, electrifying upset.

"There's no question in my mind or anyone else's mind at Miami who is No. 1," Schnellenberger declared. "The Miami Hurricanes are No. 1." Sure enough, the Hurricanes finished first in both the AP Poll and Coaches Poll.

2003 FIESTA BOWL

KEY PLAYER: CRAIG KRENZEL

TEAM: OHIO STATE BUCKEYES

OPPONENT: MIAMI HURRICANES

SETTING: TEMPE, ARIZONA, JANUARY 3, 2003

It was the last chance for Ohio State. Miami led the 2003 Fiesta Bowl 24–17 in overtime. Fourth down and goal for OSU. Quarterback Craig Krenzel fired to Chris Gamble in the right side of the end zone. Incomplete! The Miami Hurricanes won their second straight national championship!

Or did they?

Three seconds after the game was over, an official threw a yellow flag. "Hollllld the phone!" said ABC broadcaster Keith Jackson. "Everybody comes running down on the field. You've got to get off, because there's a penalty flag thrown and I think it's against Miami."

It was. The Hurricanes' Glenn Sharpe was called for pass interference against Gamble, a ruling that would be debated for years. Krenzel followed with a one-yard touchdown run, and the game went to a second overtime. What a night!

Was this the greatest college football game of all time? "It's got to be right up there if it's not," Krenzel said.

Behind freshman star running back Maurice Clarett, the OSU Buckeyes entered the Fiesta Bowl at 13–0.

Miami players celebrate "victory" in overtime after a fourth-down pass to Ohio State's Chris Gamble (7) falls incomplete. But Gamble thinks there was pass interference, and back judge Terry Porter agrees, throwing his flag.

Yet even they were an 11 ½-point underdog to 12–0 Miami, which had won 34 games in a row. Coach Larry Coker's Hurricanes featured 11 future NFL players, and their offensive line overpowered opponents. Willis McGahee (1,753 rushing yards) and Ken Dorsey (3,369 passing yards) each finished in the top five in Heisman Trophy balloting. "We were the best college team ever," McGahee said.

After a Dorsey touchdown pass opened the scoring, Krenzel and Clarett rushed for scores. Ohio State led 14–7 at the half and 17–7 late in the third quarter. At that point, the intensity heated up. McGahee ran for a touchdown with 2:24 left in the third, cutting the lead to 17–14. McGahee left the game with an injury, and for the rest of regulation each team struggled to score.

OSU running back Maurice Clarett rushes five yards for a touchdown in the second overtime. The Hurricanes still had a chance to tie, but their drive fell just short.

In the fourth quarter, Miami's Todd Sievers missed a 54-yard field goal. Then OSU's Mike Nugent blew a 42-yard field goal try. The 'Canes moved the ball to the Ohio State 31, but Roscoe Parrish fumbled. Then the Buckeyes punted, and Parrish redeemed himself. The five-foot-nine speedster returned the punt 50 yards. With 0:03 remaining in the fourth quarter, Sievers also found redemption. His 40-yard field goal tied the score at 17–17 and sent the game into overtime.

In college OT, each team gets the ball on the opponent's 25-yard line. Miami went first and scored on a touchdown pass to tight end Kellen Winslow II, son of the legendary NFL tight end. Miami led 24–17, but the Buckeyes got their chance at the 25. They eventually moved the ball to the 5, where they faced fourth-and-three. That's when Sharpe was called for interference against Gamble. "He was holding me," Gamble said of Sharpe. "He was in my facemask and my shoulder pads."

Krenzel's run and the extra point tied the score at 24–24. In the second OT, OSU scored on a five-yard run by Clarett. Now down 31–24, the 'Canes needed a touchdown and an extra point to stay alive. They made it to first-and-goal at the 2-yard-line but couldn't crack the goal line. Dorsey's incomplete pass on fourth down ended the game.

"That's what a national championship game should look like," Ohio State coach Jim Tressel said. "Double overtime. Two great heavyweights slugging it out."

And both teams thinking they won the game.

2006 ROSE BOWL

KEY PLAYER: VINCE YOUNG

TEAM: TEXAS LONGHORNS

OPPONENT: USC TROJANS

SETTING: PASADENA, CALIFORNIA, JANUARY 4, 2006

At the 2005 Heisman Trophy ceremony, USC's Reggie Bush and Texas star Vince Young anxiously awaited the announcement. Young felt he would win the award, given to college football's best player. When Bush was announced the winner, Young was not happy. He told *Texas Monthly*: "I texted and chatted with a couple of guys to let them know how I was feeling: 'It's time to go play ball and show the world that they made a mistake.'"

Young and Bush would face each other in their next game. And it wasn't *a* game. It was *the* game. In fact, many called it the most anticipated game in college football history.

Both of these teams were powerhouses. Upbeat coach Pete Carroll had led USC to 34 consecutive wins and the previous two national championships. In 2005, the electrifying Bush rushed for 1,740 yards while averaging 8.7 yards per carry. Quarterback Matt Leinart—the 2004 Heisman Trophy winner—threw for 3,815 yards in '05. The Trojans averaged 49.1 points per game, second most in the country. They were ranked number one all season.

USC running back LenDale White scores his third touchdown of the day, tying the score at 23–23 late in the third quarter. The Trojans would go up 38–26 before Vince Young orchestrated a mighty Texas comeback.

Meanwhile, Texas had won 19 straight games and was ranked number two the entire year. The Longhorns led the nation with 50.1 points per game. Young, a tremendous dual-threat quarterback, threw for 3,036 yards and rushed for 1,050.

The 2006 Rose Bowl would determine the national champion. An estimated 35.6 million viewers tuned in, making it the most watched college football game ever. Fans expected a shoot-out, and they were not disappointed.

Through three quarters, USC led 24–23. LenDale White, a huge 240-pound running back, scored three touchdowns for the Trojans. In the fourth quarter, the superstars emerged. Bush raced 26 yards for a score. After a Texas field goal made it 31–26 Texas, Leinart hit Dwayne Jarrett with a 22-yard TD pass. The Longhorns, now down 38–26 late in the fourth quarter, were in trouble.

Young, though, was determined to prevail. With 4:03 remaining, he ran 17 yards for his second rushing touchdown of the day. The extra point made it 38–33. Then, with 2:13 to go, USC's Carroll took a gamble. He went for it on fourth-and-two at the Texas 45. But the Longhorns stuffed White, giving Young a shot to win the game. Young completed four passes and carried twice. With 0:19 remaining, Texas had the ball fourth-and-five at the USC 8-yard line.

The "Game of the Century" now came down to one play. What would Vince Young do? If he ran it into the end zone, he would finish the game with 200 rushing

On fourth down with just seconds remaining, Vince Young races to the end zone for the winning touchdown. The "Game of the Century" lived up to all the hype.

yards—almost unheard of for a quarterback.

Young dropped back to pass but found no one open, so once again he tucked the ball and ran. "He's going for the corner...He's got it!" blared ABC broadcaster Keith Jackson. Texas fans went wild while the Longhorn mascot hugged the hero. Young then ran it in on the two-point conversion for a 41–38 lead, and soon the clock expired.

In celebration, confetti fell from the sky and the Longhorns' band blared "The Eyes of Texas." Though Young hadn't won the Heisman, he did earn a crystal trophy as the Rose Bowl MVP. "Don't you think that's beautiful?" he said. "It's coming home all the way to Austin, Texas."

Finally, he was happy.

2007 FIESTA BOWL

KEY PLAYER: IAN JOHNSON

TEAM: BOISE STATE BRONCOS

OPPONENT: OKLAHOMA SOONERS

SETTING: GLENDALE, ARIZONA, JANUARY 1, 2007

Boise State running back Ian Johnson had a plan. After the Fiesta Bowl, he was going to propose marriage to his girlfriend, Crissy Popadics, the captain of Boise State's cheerleading squad. But first, he had a game to win. And oh man, what a game it was!

Boise State, a school in Idaho known for its blue playing field, went 12–0 during the regular season. But as a Western Athletic Conference team, the Broncos were not eligible to play in the BCS National Championship Game. (Only schools from the 10 biggest conferences were eligible.) Oklahoma (11–2) entered the Fiesta Bowl as a seven-point favorite. The Sooners featured fast and powerful Adrian

Peterson, who would become the premier running back in the NFL.

Midway through the third quarter, BSU's Marty Tadman returned an interception 27 yards for a touchdown. Now down 28–10, the Sooners needed to shift the momentum—and that they did. Peterson soon scored on an eight-yard touchdown run, and a field goal cut the deficit to 28–20.

Late in the fourth quarter, the zaniness began. With 1:26 remaining, Oklahoma quarterback Paul Thompson

Boise State wide receiver Jerard Rabb completes the "Circus" play by diving into the end zone. The extra point made the score 35–35 with seven seconds remaining.

tossed a five-yard TD pass to make it 28–26. On the two-point conversion, penalties were called on the first two plays. During the third play, Thompson connected with Juaquin Iglesias in the end zone to tie the game.

On the next play from scrimmage, Boise State quarterback Jared Zabransky threw an interception to Marcus Walker. Stunningly, he returned it 34 yards for a touchdown. Down 35–28, the Broncos now needed a touchdown to tie. "It would have been easy to give up on us with a minute left, but we had a lot of magic left," Zabransky said.

With 18 seconds remaining, the Broncos faced fourth-and-18 at the 50. BSU head coach Chris Petersen called for the "Circus" play. Zabransky fired the ball at the 35 to Drisan James, who lateralled to Jerard Rabb. Rabb sprinted down the left sideline and dove into the end zone. This game was going to overtime!

As you will recall, during college OT each team gets a chance to score from the opponent's 25-yard line. Oklahoma simply gave the ball to Peterson, who blasted 25 yards for a touchdown. The extra point made it 42–35. BSU needed a TD and an extra point to tie.

The Broncos moved the ball to the 5-yard line but faced fourth-and-two. Time for another trick play, and this one was unusual in three ways. Wide receiver Vinny Perretta a) lined up as a running back, b) took the snap, and c) threw a touchdown pass to tight end Derek Schouman.

After scoring the winning touchdown of this extraordinary game, Boise State tailback Ian Johnson asks girlfriend Chrissy Popadics to marry him. She says yes, completing the fairy tale.

BSU decided to go for two points to win the game. Now it was Ian Johnson's time to shine. Zabransky dropped back to pass. While looking to throw, he handed the ball behind him to Johnson in the old Statue of Liberty play. Johnson ran untouched into the end zone for a 43–42 victory and a perfect 13–0 season.

Amid the on-field celebration, Johnson got on one knee to propose to Popadics. "There was no better time," he later explained. The whole proposal was shown on television. "She said yes!" said on-field FOX reporter Chris Myers. "Ian Johnson proposing to the head cheerleader at Boise State. Does it get any better than this in college football?"

2013 "IRON BOWL"

KEY PLAYER: CHRIS DAVIS
TEAM: AUBURN TIGERS
OPPONENT: ALABAMA CRIMSON TIDE
SETTING: AUBURN, ALABAMA, NOVEMBER 30, 2013

On November 18, 2013, Auburn defeated Georgia on an incredible play. Trailing 38–37 with 0:36 to go, Auburn's Nick Marshall fired a long fourth-down pass into the chest of a Bulldog defender. Dubbed the "Immaculate Deflection," the ball popped up and was grabbed by the Tigers' Ricardo Louis, who took it in for a 73-yard touchdown.

Two weeks later, Auburn prevailed in another miraculous finish—this one even more unbelievable. And it happened against its fiercest rival.

Under coach Nick Saban, Alabama entered 2013 ranked number one in the country. The powerful Crimson Tide had

won back-to-back national championships and were rolling toward a third. On November 30, 11–0 Alabama traveled to Auburn, Alabama, to face the Tigers. This annual "Iron Bowl" is football's equivalent of a civil war. "The game is the talk of the state 365 days a year," wrote Brian Stultz of CampusInsiders.com. Auburn student Kurt Sasser said that, as a kid, he dreaded going to school if the Tigers had lost to Alabama. He knew his friends would ridicule him.

The Alabama offense lines up against Auburn in the 78th "Iron Bowl." The Crimson Tide were gunning for their fourth national championship in five years and were considered almost unbeatable. *Almost*.

Auburn went 3–9 in 2012, but the Tigers entered this game at 10–1 and ranked number four in the country. The winner would play in the SEC Championship Game. For three quarters at Jordan-Hare Stadium, 87,000 fans witnessed a thrilling battle. The quarter ended with the score tied 21–21—and the best was yet to come.

With under 11 minutes to go, Alabama quarterback A. J. McCarron connected with Amari Cooper on a 99-yard touchdown pass. Up 28–21 with 2:32 remaining, Alabama kicker Cade Foster attempted a 44-yard field goal. But he kicked it too low, and it was blocked.

Fans were on their feet as Auburn had a chance to tie. For six straight plays, All-American running back Tre Mason ran the ball. On the next play, Marshall hit a wide-open Sammie Coates for a 39-yard touchdown. The extra point tied it a 28–28 at 0:32.

With seven seconds remaining, Alabama decided to run out the clock and go to overtime. But T. J. Yeldon kept running and running. His 24-yard rush put the ball on Auburn's 38-yard line. The clock hit 0:00—meaning overtime awaited—but the officials put one second on the clock. During a time-out, Saban sent in a different kicker to try a 57-yard field goal. If he made it, freshman kicker Adam Griffith would have become a hero.

Griffith, an immigrant, couldn't believe he was in this situation. He had grown up in Poland without parents. "In Poland growing up in an orphanage, there [were] no dreams," he told ESPN. "Sometimes you go to bed hungry. You don't have anything."

It seems more like a fantasy than reality. Auburn cornerback Chris Davis returns a missed field goal attempt 109 yards for the game-ending touchdown.

Griffith gave it a mighty effort, but the ball fell a few yards short of the crossbar. Chris Davis, a speedy cornerback, caught the ball nine yards deep in the end zone. From there: magic.

Griffith sprinted down the left sideline, then toward the middle of the field. Incredibly, he motored toward the end zone with no defenders around him. "When I looked back," he recalled, "I said, 'I can't believe this.'"

Shockingly, Davis had scored on a 109-yard, game-ending touchdown. Teammates tackled him in celebration while the fans stormed the field.

Kurt Sasser held his head high after the game. The following Monday, it was *Alabama* fans who dreaded going to school.

GLOSSARY

AP Poll A poll in which Associated Press sportswriters and broadcasters vote for the top teams in college football.

BCS Bowl Championship Series; a system used from 1998 to 2013 to place college football's best teams in the top five bowl games, including the BCS National Championship Game.

Coaches Poll A poll in which active college football head coaches vote for the top teams in their sport.

David vs. Goliath A story from the Bible; David battled the giant Goliath and defeated him using only a slingshot.

dual-threat quarterback A quarterback who excels as both a passer and a runner.

First Team All-Pro Voted as the best player in the NFL at his position at the conclusion of the season; several organizations pick all-pro teams, most notably the Associated Press.

lateral To pitch, throw, or hand off the football to someone behind you.

regulation The first through fourth quarters of a football game.

safety A play in which the team with the ball is tackled in the end zone; the other teams gets two points and gets the ball kicked to them on the next play.

SEC Short for Southeast Conference.

secondary A team's defensive backfield, typically comprised of two cornerbacks and two safeties.

FURTHER READING

Books

Bryant, Howard. *The Best Legends, Games, and Teams in Football*. New York, NY: Philomel Books, 2015.

Doeden, Matt. *The College Football Championship: The Fight for the Top Spot*. Minneapolis, MN: Millbrook Press, 2016.

Rice, Jerry, and Randy Williams. *50 Years, 50 Moments: The Plays That Made Super Bowl History*. New York, NY: HarperCollins, 2015.

Wilner, Barry. *The Story of the College Football National Championship Game*. Edina, MN: ABDO Publishing, 2016.

Websites

NFL Rush

nflrush.com

Includes kids-oriented NFL stories, word games, quizzes, computer games, and tons of other fun stuff.

NFL Zone

sikids.com/nfl-zone

Sports Illustrated for Kids offers NFL stories that kids will enjoy, plus a "Cool Stuff" section, "Kid Reporter," and more.

Pro-Football-Reference.com

football-reference.com

Includes statistics on every player in NFL history. For college football stats, go to: sports-reference.com/cfb.

INDEX

A

Alabama Crimson Tide, 42–45
Arizona Cardinals, 19–21
Auburn Tigers, 42–45

B

Baltimore Colts, 7–9
Boise State Broncos, 38–41

D

Dallas Cowboys, 6, 10–13

F

Fiesta Bowl (2003), 30–33
Fiesta Bowl (2007), 38–41

G

Green Bay Packers, 10–13

I

"Iron Bowl" (2013), 42–45

M

Miami Hurricanes, 26–29, 30–33

N

Nebraska Cornhuskers, 26–29
New England Patriots, 14–17, 18, 22–25
New York Giants, 7–9, 14–17, 18
NFL Championship Game (1958), 7–9
NFL Championship Game (1967), 10–13

O

Ohio State Buckeyes, 30–33
Oklahoma Sooners, 38–41
Orange Bowl (1984), 26–29

P

Pittsburgh Steelers, 18–21

R

Rose Bowl (2006), 34–37

S

Seattle Seahawks, 22–25
Super Bowl XLII, 14–17
Super Bowl XLIII, 18–21
Super Bowl XLIX, 22–25

T

Texas Longhorns, 34–37

U

USC Trojans, 34–37